# Mystery
### at the
# Christmas
# Market

# Mystery
## at the
# Christmas
# Market

BY JANELLE DILLER

ILLUSTRATIONS BY ADAM TURNER

Published by WorldTrek Publishing

Copyright © 2015 by Pack-n-Go Girls

Printed in the USA

Visit our website at www.packngogirls.com.

This is a work of fiction. Names, characters, places, and incidents either are the product of the author's imagination or are used fictitiously. The town of Kitzbühel, Austria, is real, and it's a wonderful place to visit. Any other resemblance to actual events, locales, organizations, or persons, living or dead, is entirely coincidental and beyond the intent of either the author or the publisher.

Illustrations by Adam Turner

ISBN 978-1-936376-18-6

Cataloging-in-Publication Data available from the Library of Congress.

**To sweet Cosima, my favorite Pack-n-Go Girl in the world. Be curious. Be fearless. Expect magic wherever you travel.**

*Mystery at the Christmas Market* is the third book in the Pack-n-Go Girls Austria adventures. The first book, *Mystery of the Ballerina Ghost*, tells how Brooke and Eva first met. If you haven't read it yet, you won't want to miss it.

In the second book, *Mystery of the Secret Room*, Brooke and Eva stumble upon a secret room in Schloss Mueller that's been hidden for almost 75 years. What they discover there changes the Mueller family forever.

# Contents

# Meet the Characters

**Brooke Mason** is jazzed about visiting her Austrian friend, Eva.

**Eva Mueller** loves playing with her new American friend, Brooke.

**Will Mason** is Brooke's 17-year-old brother and loves to play soccer.

**Dusty Mason** is Brooke's 14-year-old brother. He's a crazy good skier.

The Krampus isn't the only thing to be afraid of at *The Christmas Market.*

And now, the mystery begins . . .

# Chapter 1

# The Mysterious Car

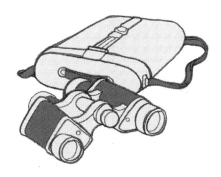

"Do you see them yet, Brooke?" Eva asked. She felt a tiny bit out of breath from running up the stairs and crawling through the wardrobe to get into their secret room in the attic.

"No. Just that black car out on the road." Brooke's nose nearly touched the frosty window.

"It's still there?"

Brooke nodded. "Did you get the binoculars?"

"Yes. But I had to sneak them out of the library.

Frau Eder was dusting in the dining room. She wouldn't be happy if she knew I brought them up here." Eva unbuckled the leather case. She carefully lifted out the antique binoculars.

"That's a cool old bag they're in," Brooke said. It reminded her of the leather on a worn horse saddle.

Eva nodded. "It's from World War II. They were my great-grandfather's from when he was in the army."

"From when the other Eva Mueller lived here and played in this room?"

Eva shook her head. "It would have been after that. That Eva would have already left Schloss Mueller with her father."

Brooke picked up the binoculars and held them up to her eyes. They weighed a ton compared to the ones her dad had back in Colorado. "They still focus great."

"Can you see anyone coming up the road?" Eva

asked her again. "Anyone? Anyone at all?"

Brooke shook her head. "Just that black car. The windows are dark. It's hard to see what's inside the car. I can make out a couple of people, though."

"What are they doing?" Eva asked.

"I can't tell."

"But why are they just sitting there by the road?"

Brooke shrugged her shoulders. "Who knows?"

"Let me see."

Eva took the binoculars from Brooke and sighed. "It's taking forever for Grandfather to pick up your dad and brothers from the airport."

"Mom said they wouldn't be here until after lunch."

"We had lunch ages ago," Eva said.

"Maybe the snow is slowing them down." Brooke could barely see the other side of the valley where the Hahnenkamm gondola carried people up to the ski slopes. "It's not snowing much here, but it looks like it's really dumping across the way. That winding road to get to Kitzbühel can be slow. Even in the summer—"

Eva touched Brooke's arm. "Wait a minute, Brooke. Those people are getting out of the car."

Even without the binoculars, Brooke could see two people step out of the car onto the snow-packed road.

"Let me see!"

Eva handed the binoculars to Brooke, who put them up to her eyes. "It's a man and a woman," Brooke said. "The man has bright red hair. Crazy red. I can see that from here. The woman is wearing a red scarf around her neck."

Brooke watched the woman walk around to the driver's side and join the man. They both stared up at the castle, or *Schloss*.

"She's pointing up at Schloss Mueller." Brooke

tried to focus her eyes better. "Uh oh. They have binoculars too. And they're looking up at us."

The girls scooted back from the window.

"Do you think they saw us?" Eva asked. Her heart pounded, but she didn't quite know why. After all, Brooke and she were in Schloss Mueller where they were supposed to be. The strangers were the ones doing something suspicious.

"I don't know," Brooke said. "But how could they see us? We're way up here in the attic. Do you think they can see through the window?"

Eva shrugged her shoulders. "Let me see the binoculars again." Just to be careful, she stood back from the window a foot or so. She could still see the strangers.

"What are they doing now?" Brooke asked.

"They're both pointing at the *Schloss*. They look pretty excited." Eva tried to focus the binoculars. "Uh oh. The lady took out a camera.

She's taking pictures of the *Schloss.*"

Both the girls shuffled another half step back from the window.

"The lady moved away from the car. Now she's almost to the lane."

"Is she still taking pictures?" Brooke asked.

Eva nodded. "It looks like it."

"Hey, is that your grandfather's car coming up the road?" Brooke asked. She stepped closer to the window again and pointed down the mountain.

Eva swung the binoculars down the winding road that led up to Schloss Mueller. "I think so." She watched the car make its way up the snowy road.

# The Mysterious Car

Each turn brought the car closer to the lane and to the castle.

"The man is getting in the car," Brooke said. "They must have heard your grandfather's car coming."

Eva shifted the binoculars back to the black car. "The woman is hurrying to get in the car, but she caught her scarf on something. Like the bumper of the car or hood. I can't tell." Eva watched the woman tug a couple of times and then yank hard on her scarf. Whatever had been caught came loose.

"She's jumping in the car now and he's taking off. Her door isn't even shut."

They watched the car pick up speed. It slid around the first corner. The car did a tiny zigzag in the snow, and then it disappeared behind some trees.

Eva put down the binoculars. "What do you think is going on?" she asked.

"I don't know," Brooke said. "But whatever it is, it isn't something good."

# Chapter 2

# The Masons Arrive!

"Dad! Will and Dusty!" Brooke threw her arms around her dad and then hugged her brothers. It had been less than a week since she'd seen them in Colorado, but she was so excited that they all finally made it to Austria for the first time. She couldn't wait for them to meet Eva and to show them Schloss Mueller.

Eva hung back on the steps that led up to the front door.

## The Masons Arrive!

Brooke couldn't remember her friend ever being this shy. She was usually the brave one. Or crazy one, depending on how you saw it. Whether they were looking for a ballerina ghost or sneaking up to their secret playroom, Eva always led the way.

"Eva, this is my dad, and these are my brothers, Will and Dusty. Will is seventeen and Dusty is fourteen. They're both in high school already." Her brothers should have done the polite thing and greeted Eva. Instead, they looked up, up, up at the windows and pale stones of Schloss Mueller.

"Wow. Super cool!" Will said. He finally remembered his manners. He brought his eyes down to greet Eva. "Hey, it's nice to finally meet you, Eva. Brooke's been telling us about all your wild adventures."

Eva smiled and politely shook hands with everyone. Her sky blue sweater matched her blue eyes. She ran her fingers through her blond curls.

"It's nice to meet you both, too. Welcome to Schloss Mueller. We're glad you can be in Austria for Christmas."

"Brooke told us your English is perfect," Dusty said. "She wasn't kidding."

Eva's cheeks grew pink. "Well, Brooke's German is getting pretty good."

Herr Mueller, Eva's grandfather, opened the trunk of the car. They all grabbed their bags and carried them inside. Mrs. Mason met them at the door with hugs and kisses. "The girls are hoping you boys will be ready to ski with them tomorrow."

"If we can stay awake, that sounds like a plan," Will said. He looked as tired as Brooke always felt after the long trip from Colorado.

Brooke waved her brothers up the grand stairway in the entrance. "I want to show you your room. You're going to love staying here. It's so beautiful."

## The Masons Arrive!

Will stared up the flights of stairs and to the high ceiling above them. "Well, it certainly doesn't look like home," he said.

"Look," Dusty pointed to the design in the floor. "There's the ballerina in the wood floor that Brooke told us about." He shook his head. "Amazing."

The boys carried their bags up the broad stairs and followed Brooke and Eva to their bedroom.

Dusty flopped on the first bed. He lay back on a pillow. "I think I'm going to need a little nap."

"You can't. I have to show you the secret room in the attic. You have to see everything." Brooke tugged her brother's hand. "Plus you have to meet Eva's cousin, Drew. The guy from Wyoming that I told you about. He's the one whose grandmother is the first Eva Mueller. The one this Eva Mueller," she put her arm around her friend, "is named for. Remember?"

Dusty nodded but his eyes were shut. "Drew is the guy who showed up last summer. You thought Drew was a bad guy until you found out his grandmother—the other Eva Mueller—was Herr Mueller's cousin. Eva Mueller's dad took her away from Schloss Mueller before World War II started."

"Exactly. Schloss Mueller has been in the Mueller family for hundreds of years. Hundreds." Brooke tried to pull Dusty up. "And yes. Drew is the grandson of Eva Mueller. He's older than you guys. He's really nice."

Dusty yawned.

Brooke kept tugging on her brother's arm. "You're going to really like Drew. He loves horses and skiing and mountain biking. Just like you guys."

Dusty yawned again.

"Besides, you don't want to miss a bite of Frau Eder's cooking," Brooke added. "I think she's making *Kaiserschmarrn* for dessert tonight."

"*Kaiserschmarrn*? Have we ever heard of that, Will?" Dusty sat up and looked confused.

"Maybe only 6,000 times." Will turned to Eva, who now stood waiting in the doorway. "Our little Brookie loves *Kaiserschmarrn*. Yes, she does."

Brooke put her fists on her hips. "That's not true. I haven't talked about *Kaiserschmarrn* more than ten times."

"More like ten times a day," Dusty said.

Brooke laughed and playfully punched her brother's arm. She had missed her brothers. "Come on. We want to show you the secret room before it gets too dark."

The four of them paraded up to the next floor and then up yet one more. They opened the door to the attic stairs and hiked the final steps into the open room.

The space still felt a little spooky to Brooke. It always looked like someone could be hiding behind the boxes or under the sheets that covered the furniture. Even now, months later, she got goosebumps thinking about the ballerina ghost since this is where Brooke first saw her.

"What a great place," Will said. "A little higher ceiling and we could play basketball up here." He did a jump shot with a pretend ball. The wooden floor creaked when he landed.

"Where's this secret room?" Dusty asked. He

yawned and stretched his arms and back.

"In here." Eva opened the wardrobe door. She pushed back the coats and pulled open the short door at the back.

"Through there?" Will asked. "I'm too big. I'll get stuck."

"No, you won't, silly. If Frau Eder can get through here, you can too," Brooke said. She shoved him in the direction of the wardrobe.

The four of them crawled through the doorway and into the narrow passageway.

"Keep going," Brooke told her brothers. "You'll be able to stand up again when you turn the corner."

"Awesome!" Dusty said. He looked the tiny room over. "And you found this, Brookie girl?"

Brooke smiled and nodded. "When we were playing hide and seek last summer. Eva didn't even know it was here." She loved this little room with its kid-sized table, chairs, and dresser. Since finding the room, they had played up here a dozen times. It was even better now because Frau Eder had washed the tablecloth and curtains for them, so the room looked cheerful. Somewhere Frau Eder had also found a set of play dishes.

"And look," Eva took out a box of fake desserts, fruits, and vegetables. "Frau Eder helped us make these out of glue, flour, and food coloring." She offered a frosted cupcake to Dusty that looked real enough to eat.

"Yum, yum, yum. Delicious!" Dusty said. He smacked his lips and pretended to eat the cupcake. "I can see why you talked so much about this place when you got home last summer, Brookie." He walked over to the window. "Wow! Great view!" It had stopped snowing, and the air had cleared. The winter sun peaked through the clouds. Fresh snow sparkled like diamonds in the soft afternoon light.

"Is that where we're skiing tomorrow?" Dusty asked. He pointed to the ski slopes across the valley.

Eva nodded. "They do World Cup races on those slopes. It's the best skiing in the world."

Dusty shook his finger. "Except for Colorado."

"We'll see about that," Eva said and laughed.

"Thanks for the tour. And now, I want to

head back downstairs," Will said. "I want to take a shower before dinner."

"I want you to take a shower before dinner, too," Dusty said.

Will rolled his eyes, but he laughed. The boys headed back through the narrow passageway and through the wardrobe.

Eva put the fake cupcake into the box and put it back in the drawer. "I like your brothers," she said to Brooke.

"I do too." Brooke loved that she could share the fun of Austria with Will and Dusty. She smiled. "Even if they tease me way too much, they take good care of me." She sighed. "This is a perfect day."

Eva shook her head no. "Not perfect yet."

Brooke looked at her.

"It'll be perfect when my mom and dad get here the day after tomorrow.

## The Masons Arrive!

Brooke thought about her own family. She saw her mom and dad almost every day of the year. Her brothers were crazy. Will sometimes acted like her dad instead of her brother, which was annoying. Dusty teased her all the time. All. The. Time. That was annoying, too. Brooke loved her grandparents, and they totally loved her like Herr Mueller loved Eva. But what if she only saw her grandparents and not the rest of her family?

Brooke nodded. "I think I can understand, Eva. Tell me again why your mom and dad are gone so much. I forget."

Eva sighed and sat down on a chair at the small table. "They own a company that makes the best chocolates in the world." She paused and then smiled. "Well, at least the best chocolates in Austria." Her eyes got watery. "They have to travel all the time. They're always off buying cocoa or setting up more stores around Europe."

Eva put her elbows on the table and rested her chin on her hands. "Do you want to know what I want for Christmas?"

Brooke shook her head. This trip to Austria was her family's Christmas present. And everyone's birthday present. And Mother's Day and Father's Day presents. And everything else present for the whole next year. And maybe the next. She was perfectly happy with that.

"Here's what I want for Christmas," Eva said. "I just want my mom and dad to be home all the time and never, ever leave again. That's all. No one even has to wrap that present." She looked up at Brooke. "But that'll never happen."

"It could happen," Brooke said. She really wanted her friend not to be so sad.

Eva shook her head and sighed again. "We probably ought to head downstairs for dinner."

Brooke looked around the room one last time

and saw the binoculars. "Uh oh. How are we going to get these downstairs again?"

Eva scrunched up her nose. "Maybe we can wait till tomorrow. I don't think anyone will notice they're gone tonight."

"Let's hope." Brooke picked up the binoculars and looked out the window. She took a quick breath. "Oh, no."

"What?"

"I can't believe it."

"Can't believe what?" Eva asked.

"They're back."

"Who? The black car with the two people?"

Brooke nodded. "And they're taking pictures again."

# Chapter 3

# The Discovery

The snow crunched beneath Brooke's ski boots. She loved that sound. It reminded her of winter, of fun times skiing with her brothers, of everything she loved about Colorado.

Drew, Will, and Dusty crept along in front of them. Their boots crunched too.

They all moved closer to the gondola. The many lines of people kept squeezing into fewer and fewer lines. Brooke tried to stay close to her brothers. The crowding in felt so unlike the tidy mazes the Colorado ski areas used. It made her nervous she'd lose Will and Dusty.

Suddenly, Eva whispered, "Brooke, look ahead."

Brooke looked up. "Huh?"

"The Reds." Eva nodded toward the people ahead of and over from them.

Brooke looked past her brothers and Drew. She looked past the family from Japan in front of the boys. And there they were. The man with the crazy red hair and the woman with the red scarf.

She took in a sharp breath and looked at Eva. "What are they doing here?" she whispered. "Do they know we're here?"

Eva whispered back, "Pretty creepy."

They all trudged forward.

"Can you hear what they're saying, Eva?"

Eva shook her head no.

A gondola arrived. The Reds just missed getting in.

The next gondola rounded the corner and slowed down.

The Reds climbed in.

The Japanese family followed.

The gondola had room for two more.

"You guys go and wait for us at the top," Will said to Brooke and Eva. "Drew, Dusty, and I want to ride together."

Eva looked at Brooke. She looked as nervous as Brooke felt. "They don't know about the Reds," Eva whispered.

The boys helped the girls put their skis in the ski holders on the outside of the gondola. Drew gave a hand to Eva and then Brooke as they stepped in. The Japanese family sat across from them. They faced the uphill direction. Eva sat next to the man with the crazy red hair. They all faced downhill.

The gondola lifted off the ground and glided

up toward the mountaintop. The village grew farther and farther away.

"Gorgeous day, isn't it?" the woman with the red scarf asked in English.

The Japanese family nodded and smiled. Brooke didn't think they understood.

Eva said, *"Bitte?"*

Brooke knew that *bitte* meant please. She also knew that Austrians said *bitte* when they didn't understand, even though Eva understood perfectly.

"Beautiful day for skiing, isn't it?" the man with the red hair said.

The Japanese family smiled again. They definitely didn't understand English.

*"Bitte?"* Eva said again. She poked Brooke in the ribs.

Brooke got the signal. Eva didn't want her to talk.

"You don't speak English?" the woman with

the red scarf asked. She raised her eyebrows.

The Japanese family smiled even bigger.

Eva poked Brooke in the ribs again. She smiled at the woman with the red scarf and shrugged.

Brooke tried not to look at anyone. She was a lousy liar.

The gondola traveled higher and higher. Below them, trees and skiers grew smaller and smaller. The view across the valley rose in front of them. It took Brooke's breath away. She could see the jagged peaks of the Wilde Kaiser mountain range in the distance. She could also see across to the other mountain, the Kitzbüheler Horn. Even though she'd ridden tons of ski lifts and gondolas in Colorado, she never got tired of the views.

"Look, Paul," the woman with the red scarf said. "We can see it from here." She pointed across the valley. "Terrific view, isn't it?"

Brooke followed the direction she pointed.

## The Discovery

Schloss Mueller! She grabbed Eva's hand. Eva glanced at her out of the corner of her eye. She knew too.

The man with the red hair nodded. He pulled out his binoculars and looked. "It's perfect," he said.

The woman with the red scarf dug through her backpack. She pulled out a camera and started snapping pictures. Most of the pictures seemed to be in the direction of Schloss Mueller.

Snap, snap snap. Snap. Snap.

The woman with the red scarf finally put down her camera. "I think these little girls are perfect. What do you think?" she said to the man with the crazy red hair.

The little girls are perfect? It took Brooke a second to realize the woman was talking about Eva and her.

"Yeah. I love the contrast. A blondie and a kid with black hair and a little color to her skin. One looks Austrian and the other . . ."

Brooke waited to hear how he would describe her. They'd never guess her grandma was Native American. Most people thought she looked Mexican.

The woman in the red scarf finished. "She looks like she could be from anywhere."

Brooke squeezed Eva's hand. Hard.

"Okay, we have the place and the kids," said the man. "Now we need the where and the when."

"And the how much," the woman added.

# The Discovery

How much?

It finally fell into place.

The Reds were kidnappers! Brooke couldn't believe what she was hearing. Her heart pounded so loudly in her chest that she was sure everyone in the gondola could hear.

Eva dug her elbow deeper into Brooke's side. She was sure she'd have a black and blue spot from it.

"We're going to have to think about how much to ask," the man said. "We can't be stupid and ask too much. But we also can't ask too little. Or no one will take it seriously."

"That's going to take some thought," the woman said. "We don't have to figure that out yet. I'm more worried about where we grab them."

"I've got it," the red-haired man said. "The *Christkindlmarkt*. The Christmas Market. It's perfect. Lots of stuff going on. Lots of people. They'd be easy to snatch."

Brooke stared out the window. How could these people be so bold? How could they talk so easily about kidnapping Eva and her?

Eva pressed her elbow in again.

"We use the whole *Krampus* thing," the woman said.

*"Krampus?"* The man tilted his head.

"Yeah. You know. The Austrian tradition. The beast-like creatures. They punish children who aren't good. They're all over the Austrian Christmas markets."

Brooke tried to look at Eva's face. She'd never heard of a *Krampus*.

Eva didn't look at her, but her eyes were big. They were both thinking the same thing.

"Right. They have brooms and chains and horns and stuff," the man said. "It's a great idea. The Christmas markets have dozens of people wearing *Krampus* masks. It'll be easy to escape."

Brooke didn't think she was even breathing. But

she had to hear every single word.

"But how do we know the girls will be at the Christmas Market?" the red-haired man asked.

"Good question. We have to figure that part out. Every Austrian family goes to the Christmas Market at least one night," the woman with the red scarf said.

"It'll happen early because the girls can't be out late," the man said. "We won't have to wait long."

"Exactly."

Brooke's heart felt like a hammer pounding in her chest.

The gondola slowed as it neared the station. In a minute, they'd all step out and ski away like nothing happened.

Only everything had happened.

# Chapter 4

# The Chase

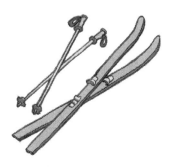

Eva said something in German that Brooke didn't understand. She caught the word "ski," but that was it.

They all climbed out of the gondola. Eva lifted her skis out of the holder. She waited just long enough for the Reds to grab their stuff. Then she took off after them.

"Brooke, *komm*!" Eva called back over her shoulder. She motioned with her head to keep moving.

"We have to wait for Drew and my brothers,"

Brooke said. She hoped the Reds were far enough in front of them that they couldn't hear. But she didn't know for sure.

"Forget them," Eva said. She dropped her skis at the first patch of snow and clicked into the bindings. "They'll have to catch up with us. We need to follow the Reds."

"What? Are you totally nuts?" Brooke couldn't believe Eva had such a crazy idea. "What do you think we can do if we catch them? Tackle them? Make them promise they won't kidnap us?"

Eva wasn't listening to her, though. "Come on!" she called back to Brooke again.

Brooke saw the gondola arrive with Drew and her brothers. The doors opened. Five other people stepped out, and then Drew, Will, and Dusty. It looked to Brooke like they moved in slow motion.

"Guys, over here," Brooke called to her brothers. She waved her hand at them to hurry up.

Eva stood at the edge of the slope fifty feet away. She already had on her skis, helmet, and goggles. She waved to Brooke, just like Brooke had waved to the boys. She yelled something, but Brooke didn't catch it. Then she spread her hands as if to say, "What's taking you so long?"

Brooke clomped over as fast as she could. She dropped her skis next to Eva.

"*Schnell!* Hurry! We're going to miss the Reds." Eva pointed down the slope with her ski pole. "They're already at the first bend. We'll lose sight of them."

"We can't leave without Drew and my brothers," Brooke said. She quickly tapped one boot with her pole and then the other boot to knock the snow off before stepping into her skis. "My mom would kill me if she thought the two of us took off on our own."

"She'll be happy if we stop the kidnappers. Won't she?" Eva didn't wait for an answer. Let's

# The Chase

go!" She pushed off and flew down the slope.

Brooke waved at her brothers again. "Hurry! I have to catch Eva!" The boys were only a few feet away, but they seemed in no hurry.

"Where's the fire, Brookie?" Will asked. He dropped his skis and reached down to tighten his boot buckles.

Brooke snapped on her helmet and pulled on her goggles. She pushed off the edge and raced after Eva. "We have to catch the woman in the red scarf. We'll wait for you at the bottom," she called back to them. And under her breath, she added, "Just don't tell Mom we didn't wait for you."

Eva had a good thirty-second lead, but Brooke skied rocket fast. At least that's what her brothers always said. She also had more nerve skiing the bumps than it looked like Eva had. The gap between them shrunk by half. Eva carved a big turn and then disappeared behind a grove of trees.

# The Chase

Seconds later, Brooke followed. The slope narrowed into a wide trail with other slopes dropping off of it. Brooke's heart sank. She couldn't see Eva's pink jacket anywhere. She skied to the side and stopped to look for the boys. If they missed the turn, she would be in a mess of trouble.

She pushed herself forward with her poles. She came to the first slope that dropped off from the trail. It was steep and full of bumps. If Eva had taken it, Brooke thought she'd still be able to see her. The second slope looked easier, but it turned behind some trees pretty quickly. Eva could be long gone down that slope and Brooke would never know.

She moved on toward the third slope.

Will skied up beside Brooke. "What do you think you're doing skiing away like that?" He sounded super annoyed.

"No kidding," Dusty added. He had skied up on the other side of her. "You know better than that.

Mom's going to be one unhappy camper when she finds out. She'll never let you go with just us again."

"I know, I know, I know," Brooke said. "It's just that—" They reached the third slope that dropped off of the trail. "There she is! Eva!" Brooke yelled down the slope. She pushed herself ahead of her brothers and turned her skis downhill.

Eva turned to look up the slope. When she saw Brooke, she waved her ski pole. Brooke flew down the slope and pulled up to a flying stop next to Eva.

"We lost them," Eva said. She looked grim. "I think they must have taken one of the other slopes."

Will and Dusty both zoomed toward them. At the last second, they turned and slid to a quick stop beside the girls.

"What's going on?" Will asked. "Are you nuts? You know you're supposed to stick with us. What if we'd lost you?"

"I know," Brooke said. She sighed. How could

she ever explain this to her brothers?

"We were trying to catch the kidnappers," Eva said.

"The what?" Will asked.

"The kidnappers," Eva said again.

"Kidnappers?" Drew said as he skied to a stop beside the others.

"Yes. Kidnappers," Eva said. "We saw them watching Schloss Mueller yesterday. Then today we rode in the same gondola. We heard them talking about kidnapping us!"

Will and Dusty looked at each other. They burst out laughing. "Ballerina ghosts and now kidnappers," Will said. "Eva, you've been hanging out too long with Brookie girl. Our baby sister has a wild imagination."

"Let's go, you guys," Dusty said. "This time stick with us, girls. We've got miles to ski before we sleep."

Drew and Will pushed off and headed down

the mountain. Snow flew from their skis.

"But we heard them—" Brooke began.

"No buts." Dusty turned his skis downhill and took some air on the first bump. Another couple of bumps later he threw a flip, aced the landing, and threw his arms straight up in the air. "Whoohoo!" he shouted.

"Now what?" Eva asked Brooke.

"I don't know," Brooke muttered. She slid forward on her skis. "But we've got to figure out a way to convince them we're not crazy."

Far, far down the slope, the girls spotted a red-haired man and a woman with a cherry red scarf glide out of the trees and fly on down the mountain.

## Chapter 5

# Not the Christkindlmarkt!

Brooke and Eva lugged their boots and skis into Schloss Mueller. They shook the snow off their jackets and hung them up to dry.

"Good day, Brookie girl?" Dusty playfully tugged Brooke's ponytail.

"Yup. A good day." And it was good except for one thing. The boys still didn't believe there were kidnappers on the loose. In fact, it had gotten worse as the day went on. Every time one of the boys spotted anything red, they yelled, "Kidnapper alert!" And then they would laugh and laugh.

Unfortunately, it seemed every skier wore a red jacket, hat, or scarf that day.

By lunchtime, Brooke and Eva began to wonder, too. Maybe it had just been their imaginations.

Except they had heard the Reds in the gondola. They'd seen them on the road. Twice.

It couldn't be just their imaginations.

Frau Eder came out of the kitchen with a tray full of cups and two pots with something steaming. "Hot chocolate or coffee?" she asked. "The *Stollen* is already in the library." She motioned with her head to follow her.

Mrs. Mason helped her with the tray and started pouring hot cocoa into the cups. Herr Mueller handed one to each of the girls. Mr. Mason poured coffee for the rest and handed the steaming cups around. Frau Eder placed the sliced *Stollen* onto plates and handed the fruity Christmas bread around.

Brooke breathed in the rich chocolate scent. She let the steam warm her face before she took her first sip. "Mmmmmm," she said. "I could sit in this cozy chair all day and watch the snow."

"*Ja,*" Herr Mueller said. "It is perfect, isn't it?"

"*Nein, Grossvater,*" Eva said. "Tomorrow will be perfect."

Herr Mueller laughed. "Yes, *Liebling.* It will be more perfect when our family is together." He set his cake plate down. "But for tonight, I have a special surprise. I've ordered a taxi van. We're going to the *Christkindlmarkt,* the Christmas market in Kitzbühel."

The girls looked at each other. Brooke shuddered. She whispered to Eva. "Not the *Christkindlmarkt.* Not tonight."

"I know!" Eva whispered back. "The kidnappers."

"Wonderful idea, Herr Mueller," Mrs. Mason said. "We have Christmas markets in the US, but they're copied after the German and Austrian ones. I can't wait to see the real thing." She turned to Brooke and Eva and the boys. "You all go get cleaned up."

"Uh, Mom," Brooke began. "We're really tired." She looked at Eva, who nodded her head. "We think we'll just stay home."

Will cleared his throat. "Brookie, you don't have to worry. I'm sure the Reds won't be at the *Christkindlmarkt*. They're tired from skiing all day." He winked at Dusty. "And looking for little girls to kidnap."

"Huh?" Mrs. Mason jerked her head and looked at Will.

Dusty laughed and wiggled a fork at Brooke. "I

don't know. The Reds could be driving up the road right now to grab you."

Brooke's face felt hot. This kind of teasing wasn't fun. Especially in front of everyone. And even more especially because now her mom really wouldn't believe her. "But Mom," she said. "There really are kidnappers. Eva and I rode up in the gondola with two Americans. They talked about kidnapping us."

Mrs. Mason gave Brooke a funny look. Then she waved her hand. "Nonsense. I'm sure you must have misunderstood." She gave Brooke a little hug. "You don't want to miss the *Christkindlmarkt*, do you? It's really special. We'll go early. You can come home and go straight to bed." She shooed them upstairs to go change their clothes.

"What are we going to do?" Brooke asked as she put on a clean sweater and jeans. "What if the kidnappers are there, and they really DO kidnap us?"

"It'll be just like the first Eva Mueller," Eva said. Brooke thought she sounded like she might cry. "She didn't even get to say goodbye to anyone. Her father just snatched her and took her to the United States forever."

"Well, he left because he was mad at his father. These kidnappers will ask for a ransom." Brooke felt close to tears, too. "Your grandfather and my mom and dad would pay a ransom. I'm sure of it."

## Not the Christkindlmarkt!

"But what if—" Eva stopped. "What if something happens and we can't come back? I'll never see my mom and dad again."

"You mean, what if we accidentally—" Brooke couldn't bring herself to say the word "die."

Eva nodded. She threw her arms around Brooke and hugged her. "No matter what, we have to stick together."

Brooke nodded. "And we hang on to my mom and dad and your grandfather."

"We never let go. No matter what."

"Girls?" Mrs. Mason called up the stairs. "Are you ready?"

"In a minute, Mom."

They hugged one more time and then headed toward the stairs.

"Wait a minute, Brooke," Eva said. She dashed back to her room. Seconds later, she returned. She held a silver locket in her hands, the locket the other

47

Eva Mueller had left in the secret room when her father took her away. Eva clicked open the heart-shaped locket. The girls looked at the two pictures inside one more time. One side held a picture of Herr Mueller's mother when she was a young woman. On the other side was a photo of the first Eva Mueller. She looked about nine-years old in the picture. But it had been taken almost seventy-five years earlier. "The first Eva Mueller didn't have time to take this. We're not making the same mistake."

# Chapter 6

# The Escape

No one noticed how quiet Brooke and Eva were in the car.

No one heard their hearts pounding.

No one saw their eyes grow big when they drove around the curve and saw the big black car. The taxi driver gave a friendly wave to the other driver. He had crazy red hair.

"Tonight's the night," Brooke whispered. She

squeezed Eva's hand. Eva squeezed back.

"We stick together. No matter what," Eva whispered back.

Brooke twisted around to see if the black car had turned around to follow them.

For a moment, she only saw the empty road. The full moon shone on the snow, making the shadows black and the moonlit areas white. Then headlights swept around the curve.

"They're following us," she whispered to Eva.

"Are you sure it's them?" Eva asked. She turned to look.

"I can't tell for sure, but I'm betting it is. Who else would be on the road now?"

The adults and boys chatted away.

No one cared about the black car following them.

No one noticed the girls whispering.

No one thought to ask the girls why they looked so nervous.

# The Escape

They wound their way down the curvy mountain road and into the village. The taxi van dropped them off a short block from the entrance to the old part of town. The girls watched the black car drive on past. The woman with the red scarf pointed at them as they drove by.

Brooke zipped up her ski jacket and grabbed her mother's hand as soon as she stepped on the street. Eva held on to Brooke.

"Mom," Brooke said and tugged on her mother's hand. "The Reds just drove by."

"What, dear?" Mrs. Mason leaned down.

"The kidnappers just drove by," Brooke said again.

"Oh, sweetheart. You have such a fun imagination." Mrs. Mason squeezed Brooke's hand and pulled her toward the market.

Brooke looked at Eva and sighed a heavy sigh.

Tiny white lights decorated shop windows and

trees. Beyond them, the old stone arch entrance to the village looked pretty as a postcard. Brooke could see the snowy street and a horse-drawn carriage. She could hear the jingle of the bells on the horse as it stamped its feet.

The village truly felt magical. Small wooden stands lined both sides of the street. One was filled with Christmas angels of every size. Another had gingerbread hearts, and another sold giant pretzels. Still another had shelves of painted wooden ornaments. A brass quintet played on an open balcony above the market. Brooke loved the trumpet's clear, pure sound. The music seemed to gently fall on the street below. Christmas trees with more tiny white lights dotted the open spaces between booths.

"That's 'Silent Night,' isn't it?" Brooke said to Eva.

"Yes, it's '*Stille Nacht*.' You know this song?"

Eva asked. She sounded surprised.

"Sure. It's very familiar. We sing it every Christmas."

"It was written by an Austrian almost 200 years ago," Eva said.

"Nice." Brooke liked that she'd been singing an Austrian song every Christmas for as long as she could remember.

"Brooke, you have to try one of these," Eva said. She tugged her friend over to a booth that had a beautiful spread of cookies.

Brooke pulled her mom over to the booth, too.

"See these?" Eva pointed at some cookies frosted with powdered sugar and shaped into crescents. "They're *Vanillekipferl*." The powdery white cookies looked like silvery white quarter moons next to the gingerbread hearts.

Mrs. Mason took out some euros and bought a plate of cookies.

# Mystery at the Christmas Market

# The Escape

"Can you taste the *mandeln*? I don't know what the English word is," Eva said.

"*Mandeln* must mean almonds. At least that's what I smell." Brooke breathed in the scent.

"That's it. Almonds," Eva said. She took a bite of the crumbly cookie. "It's heavenly, isn't it?"

Brooke nodded.

"Frau Eder makes the cookies and then makes us wait two whole days to eat them. She says that's what makes them crumbly."

"This just might be better than *Kaiserschmarrn*," Brooke said. She took another cookie from the plate.

Giant snowflakes fell lightly around them. Brooke breathed in the crisp air. She smelled grilling bratwurst and something else. Something cinnamon and sweet. "What's that smell?" she asked Eva.

"That's *gluhwein*," Eva said. "It's a warm Christmas drink for adults that smells spicy. Kids

drink *Kinderpunsch*, which is a hot mulled cider."
She sniffed the air. "They say that it's not a true
*Christkindlmarkt* unless it touches every sense. You
have to see, taste, smell, hear, and touch something
special."

"Then this is a true *Christkindlmarkt*," Brooke
said as she brushed her hand over a display of
shiny silver bells.

They strolled past a Christmas tree with
delicate white lights. The tree stretched all the way
to the third floor window. Brooke realized she'd
missed seeing a Christmas tree at Schloss Mueller.

"Why don't you have a Christmas tree?"
Brooke asked Eva.

"Oh, we will," Eva said. "We just don't see it
until the night before Christmas. We hear a tinkling
bell, and then we get to see it all decorated. It's
always so beautiful to walk in the room and see it
shining."

"But then you don't get to see your Christmas presents under the tree until the day before Christmas."

"Of course not. Why would I see presents that I can't open until Christmas?" Eva sounded confused. "Besides, I do get some small presents on December 6. That's when we put a shoe outside and it gets filled with small oranges, peanuts, and chocolates."

"A shoe?" Brooke wrinkled her nose.

Eva nodded. "You don't put a shoe out?"

Brooke shook her head and thought a minute. Then she laughed. "We put a stocking up instead of a shoe."

"How funny," Eva said. "A shoe and a sock are both Christmas traditions."

If it had been any other evening, Brooke would never want to leave this beautiful spot.

But tonight wasn't just any evening.

Tonight was the night the kidnappers planned to strike.

Tonight was maybe the last night she'd ever see her mom and dad and brothers.

She squeezed her mom's hand. Her mom squeezed back.

"Look, Brooke." Her mom let go of her hand and pulled her camera out of her pocket. She pointed at two devils with facemasks and brooms headed toward them. "It's a *Krampus*! The Austrian Christmas monster. They scare the children into being good."

The *Krampus* with the red scarf playfully bumped the people in her way. In another few feet she'd be close enough to grab them.

"The Reds!" Brooke hollered to Eva. She grabbed for her mom again. But her mom had moved to the side of the street to take a picture.

"*Lauf!* Run!" Eva shouted.

# The Escape

"Where? Where can we go?" Brooke twisted around to look for her dad or brothers. But they'd disappeared into the crowd.

Eva yanked Brooke's hand. "To the church!"

Brooke felt the broom of the *Krampus*. A hand reached for her, but she slipped away.

They ran. They ran through the crowd and up the slippery street.

"This way!" Eva tugged her friend along the cobblestone.

Brooke twisted around and looked back. She saw another *Krampus* behind them. Her heart exploded in her chest.

"Turn here." Eva pulled her along.

They ran up the stone path to the ancient cathedral. Candles sat on each step, lighting the way. Above them, the moon slipped behind a cloud.

Brooke grabbed the handle of the massive wooden door to the church. She could hear singing inside. The beautiful music made her wish she could slip inside the church and sing along with them.

"No, Brooke," Eva whispered loudly. "That's the first place they'll look. We'll hide in the *Friedhof.*"

"The what?" Brooke whispered back.

"The . . . the what do you call it? The cemetery," Eva said.

"What?" Brooke panicked. Surely Eva didn't mean what she'd just said.

# The Escape

"The cemetery? Where?"

"Here," Eva waved her hand around the church.

The moon came out from behind the cloud. Rows and rows of headstone shadows appeared around them. Each headstone sat in a little garden plot with bushes, vines, and short fences.

It was the first Brooke realized they stood in the middle of a graveyard that surrounded the church. Eva yanked Brooke behind a giant tombstone. They scooted down in the shadows.

"We'll be safe here," Eva whispered. "No one will find us."

"Unless they hear my heart pounding," Brooke whispered back.

"Or mine."

The girls held hands. Brooke didn't know who squeezed the hardest.

# Chapter 7

# Graveyard Secrets

The church clock chimed the quarter hour.

"How long do we hide here?" Brooke whispered.

"Until it's safe," Eva answered.

"I know. But does that mean we stay five minutes or till Monday?" Brooke asked.

Eva giggled.

Brooke giggled, too.

They tried to laugh quietly. But they were

both tired and scared. Giggling seemed better than crying.

"Shush." Brooke put her finger to her mouth. "We can't let them hear us."

They listened for footsteps in the snow. Music from the church spilled out into the cemetery. The brass quintet at the *Christkindlmarkt* began playing again. They played something totally different than the church song. But somehow, the two kinds of music blended. It felt soothing to Brooke.

They could barely hear the other sounds from the *Christkindlmarkt*. Every now and then, they heard a squeal. Brooke figured a *Krampus* had scared someone.

The moonlight played tricks with Brooke's eyes. She thought she saw a *Krampus* sneaking along the stonewall at the back of the cemetery. She blinked, and the *Krampus* disappeared. Another shape darted past her. Brooke froze.

"It's just a cat," Eva whispered.

"It scared me to death," Brooke whispered.

"Well, we're in the right place for that," Eva said quietly. She giggled again.

And then they heard other voices.

"Shush," Brooke said again.

A couple of people came up the stone steps. Their footsteps crunched louder on the snow.

Brooke couldn't make out the words, but she knew the voices.

Eva looked at her. She mouthed the words, "The Reds."

Neither girl breathed.

"Oh no!" Brooke whispered as quietly as she could. She poked Eva. "Your coat." She pointed to the edge of Eva's jacket. It spread out just beyond the shadow of the gravestone.

Eva quickly tucked it back in the shadow.

The girls looked at each other. They knew how

# Graveyard Secrets

close they'd come to being seen.

They heard the man's voice first. "The *Krampus* disguise is brilliant. You whip off the mask, throw a coat over the costume, and toss the broom. No one knows who the kidnapper is."

The girls froze. They didn't dare move an inch.

"And a *Krampus* wears gloves." It was the woman's voice.

"Right. No fingerprints," The man said.

The two didn't talk for a minute. Then the woman said, "Having the cemetery right next to the church is spooky, don't you think?"

"Look at all the huge gravestones," the man said. "They make a perfect hiding spot."

"Interesting," the woman said. "It looks like these are plots for generations of families, not just one person."

Footsteps crunched on the snow just on the other side of their hiding place. If the Reds took another two steps, they'd be able to see over the headstone. They'd see the girls. They could grab Brooke and Eva and no one would hear them scream.

They couldn't have picked a worse hiding place.

"So we're agreed then," the woman said. "Tonight's the night, right?"

"Agreed," the man said. "If we don't do it tonight, we might miss our chance."

"What's the name again? Miller?" the woman asked.

"No, it's . . . it's—" The man paused. "Let me check my notes." He rattled some papers. "It's Mueller."

Eva jerked her head toward Brooke. "He said Mueller," she mouthed silently. She pointed to herself.

Goosebumps marched up Brooke's arms. She felt lightheaded from what the Reds must have meant.

Brooke's nose tickled. She felt a sneeze coming on. And then it went away.

The footsteps moved away from them and farther into the cemetery. Brooke could still hear the Reds talking, but she couldn't hear what they were saying.

"What are we going to do?" Eva whispered quietly in Brooke's ear. "Run or stay?"

Brooke shrugged her shoulders. "They're too close," she whispered back. "We have to stay." Her nose tickled again. She rubbed it and hoped a sneeze wouldn't come. Not now.

The footsteps in the snow crunched closer again. The voices grew louder.

"We'll hide them in the cemetery," the woman said. "At least for a while."

"But only at night," the man said. "Too many people are here during the day."

The Reds couldn't have been more than ten steps away.

Close enough to hear their hearts pounding.

Close enough to hear a sneeze.

Brooke's nose really tickled now. She couldn't hold back the sneeze any longer. "Ahhhchoo!" She sneezed into her glove.

"What was that?" the man said.

"It sounded like a sneeze," the woman said. "It came from over there."

Footsteps crunched closer.

The girls looked at each other. Brooke had never felt so scared.

"Run?" Eva mouthed the question.

Brooke shook her head.

"Oh look," the woman said. "It's a cat. That's the sneeze we must have heard."

"You think that was a cat sneeze we heard?" the man asked. "It sounded more like a human."

"Don't be silly, Paul," the woman said. "Do you see anyone else?" She laughed lightly. "Maybe we heard a ghost."

They heard the man snort. "You know, this is a little creepy out here. Let's get out of this cemetery. Let's check out the church. And then we'll go find them in the *Christkindlmarkt*."

"We better hurry. Who knows how long they'll stay at the market," the woman said.

The two people crunched the snow as they walked past the girls' hiding place. If the man and woman listened closely enough, Brooke was sure they'd hear their hearts thump, thump, thumping.

She heard the squeak and the creak of the church door opening. For a quick moment, they saw the light from the open church door shine all the way to the stonewall.

"Now! We run!" Eva whispered and jumped up.

Brooke jumped up, too, but her knees felt cold and stiff from sitting on the snowy ground. She took a couple of steps and then stumbled over a low fence. She landed flat on her face. Her knee banged against something hard. "Ouch!"

Eva looked back, horrified. She reached down and pulled up her friend. Brooke brushed the snow off her wounded knee. She limped after Eva as fast as she could. The girls dashed to the steps and hurried down into the village.

They didn't stop until they saw a *Krampus* round the corner. This time they knew it wasn't one of the Reds.

"How long have we been gone?" Brooke asked

Eva. She tried to catch her breath. "Everyone must be frantic."

"It's been at least an hour, I'm sure," Eva said.

The church clock chimed the half hour.

Brooke looked at Eva. "Well, we've been gone at least fifteen minutes. Still, they must be really worried."

The girls turned the corner into the *Christkindlmarkt.*

"Do you see anyone we know?" Eva asked.

"Over there." Brooke pointed. "Will, Dusty, and Drew are at that pretzel stand."

The girls wove through the crowd. They dodged another *Krampus* and yet another and more brooms. They reached the boys just as Mrs. Mason did. "Oh good," Mrs. Mason said. "I've been looking for all of you. Come, girls. I want to show you this stand with the most beautiful angels." She took Brooke and Eva's hands.

"Mom," Brooke said. "We were almost kidnapped. We just barely escaped!"

"What, sweetheart?" Mrs. Mason said.

Brooke knew her mom hadn't heard her at all.

"Look," her mom said. "Don't you love these angels? They're so simple yet special."

Brooke looked at Eva.

Eva shook her head.

"What do we need to do to get them to understand?" Brooke said.

Eva sighed. "Get kidnapped, I guess."

"What, Eva?" Mrs. Mason said. "Why don't both of you pick out an angel. It'll help you remember Christmas this year."

The girls sighed. They'd have no trouble remembering Christmas this year.

If they survived it.

# Chapter 8

# The Final Escape

The taxi van wound its way up the curvy mountain road. The girls sat in the far back seat. With each turn, the lights of the town grew farther away.

"Nobody believes us," Eva said to Brooke. "Nobody."

"At least the Reds didn't find us again at the *Christkindlmarkt*," Brooke said.

"Only because we convinced Grandfather we couldn't stay awake another minute."

# The Final Escape

"It'll serve them right when we do get kidnapped," Brooke said.

"Yeah. Then they'll believe us," Eva said. "But it'll be too late."

"And then we're the ones to lose. We'll never see our families again." Brooke rubbed her knee. She would have a bruise on it from the fall in the cemetery. She hoped she wouldn't be too sore to ski again.

If she ever got to ski again.

Headlights came up behind them.

Eva turned around. "It's them again," she said. "It's the Reds."

Brooke turned around too. "Are you sure? How can you tell?" Snow covered the rear window except for where the wiper swept it clean.

"It's black and it's the same size as their car." Eva's breath fogged the window. She wiped it clear with her glove. "I can see two people in it. It has to be them."

The car drew closer. And then it slid sideways

on the snow almost to the edge of the mountain. The car stopped and slowly crawled forward.

"We need to have a plan," Brooke said.

"I know," Eva said. "The minute we walk in the door, we run up and hide in the secret room. They'll never find us there."

Brooke felt relieved. Eva had figured out the perfect solution. It could work. Maybe if the first Eva Mueller had hidden in the secret room, her father couldn't have taken her away.

The taxi van pulled into the long lane up to Schloss Mueller. It eased to a stop in front of the ancient front doors. Mr. Mason opened the door to the van and stepped out. He turned around to help Mrs. Mason. Then the boys began to climb out.

It was taking forever to get out of the van.

Headlights turned into the lane and crept up the snowy road.

"Hurry!" Brooke pushed Dusty. She couldn't

believe he could move so slowly.

"Whoa, Brookie girl," her brother said. "What's the rush? You'll just have to go to bed sooner." He stepped out of the van and stretched. It blocked Brooke from getting around him.

"It's the kidnappers! They're driving up the lane right now!" Brooke nearly shouted.

Dusty turned around and gave his sister a hand out of the van. "Well, it'll be nice to finally meet these Reds.

Think they're coming for a little dessert?" He gave a hand to Eva and helped her out next.

"You think it's funny, but you won't when they snatch us," Brooke said. She ran up the steps to Schloss Mueller and pulled open the door. Eva slipped in behind her. Just as the door closed, Brooke saw the black car stop behind the taxi van. A man with crazy red hair stepped out of the driver's side. A woman with a cherry red scarf opened the passenger door.

"*Lauf!* Run! They're here. We have to get to the secret room!" Eva shouted.

Brooke flew up the steps to the second floor. Her knee ached. The girls scrambled up another flight of stairs and then one more. The door to the attic stairs stood only a few feet away. They couldn't stop now.

The front door opened below them. They heard feet stomping off the snow and then voices.

## The Final Escape

The Reds were in the house. They were talking to Herr Mueller and Brooke's mom and dad. It all sounded so friendly, so normal.

"*Schnell!* Hurry!" Eva whispered to Brooke. "They're inside!"

"Girls?" Herr Mueller called up the stairs. "We have someone for you to meet."

"The Reds tricked them somehow!" Brooke whispered to Eva. "Keep going."

"Eva? Brooke? Come down, please, and meet our guests," Herr Mueller called again.

"What did the Reds tell him?" Eva asked. They had reached the attic door.

Only one more flight of stairs to go. They scrambled up, up, up into the open space of the attic.

Someone's feet came pounding up the stairs.

"Faster! They're right behind us, Brooke!"

Eva yanked open the wardrobe door and pushed the coats aside. She crawled through the small door. Brooke climbed into the wardrobe after her. They were seconds away from being safely hidden in the secret room.

"Brooke," Will called out to them. "Wait up. It's not what you think."

She paused and turned. Her brother came flying up the attic steps.

"Will, you can't tell the Reds where we're hiding." Brooke slipped through the door behind Eva. She pulled it shut behind her. Her knee ached. But she could finally catch her breath.

"We're safe now," Eva said.

"Unless Will leads them up here," Brooke said.

At that moment, Will tugged the small door open and poked his head in. "Brookie, Eva. Come back downstairs, you guys. You have to meet these people," he said. He crawled through the small space and joined them in the playroom.

"No, sir," Brooke said. She shook her head.

## The Final Escape

"We're not going down there. They're here to kidnap us. We're staying here till it's safe again."

"Brookie, you got the part about the kidnapping right. But it's not at all what you think," Will said. "You're going to love what you find out."

"So you believe me now? About the kidnappers?" Brooke asked.

Will nodded his head. "I get why you think they're going to kidnap you, but they're not."

Brooke crossed her arms and harrumphed. "How do you know you're not being tricked?"

Will sighed. He looked her in the eyes. "Do you trust me, Brookie?" he asked.

Brooke nodded slowly. Of course she trusted her big brother.

"Would I ever let anything happen to you?" he asked.

Brooke shook her head. Will would do anything to keep her from getting hurt.

"Then you have to trust me now. You're not in any danger."

Brooke paused for a long time. She looked at Eva, who tilted her head slightly and shrugged her shoulders.

Finally, Brooke sighed and nodded. "Eva, I think we should go downstairs and find out what's going on."

# Chapter 9

# The Perfect Day

The three of them paraded down the attic stairs, down the steps to the third floor, down the steps to the second floor, and down the grand staircase to the first floor. The Reds stood talking to Herr Mueller and Brooke's mom and dad. They were all laughing like old friends.

Herr Mueller reached his hand toward his granddaughter. "Eva and Brooke, I want you to meet Mr. and Mrs. Henley."

"The girls from the gondola!" Mrs. Henley said. Her eyes grew big.

The Reds reached out to shake hands with the girls. Eva and Brooke looked at each other. Brooke took a deep breath and nodded to Eva. They shook hands.

And nothing happened. The Reds didn't whisk them away. They didn't grab the girls, throw open the massive front door, and race out to their big black car.

They just laughed a friendly laugh.

"We're glad to finally meet you girls," Mr. Henley said. "I think we saw you both in the attic yesterday. You were watching us, right?"

Brooke nodded.

"We didn't know who it was that was looking at us," Mrs. Henley continued. "It spooked us a little." She laughed. "I guess it spooked you, too."

Eva nodded.

"How funny that you're the same two girls from the gondola. We thought you didn't speak

English, or we would have asked you then about our project."

"Your project?" Brooke asked.

"Yes," Mr. Henley said. "My wife is a screenwriter. She writes movie scripts."

"And my husband produces movies," Mrs. Henley said.

"See?" Will whispered. "I told you that you'd like this."

Brooke elbowed him to be quiet.

"We were on vacation in Kitzbühel and came up with a great idea for a movie." Mrs. Henley smiled at the girls. "The idea is a slightly scary but mostly funny story. It's about a couple who run out of money on vacation. So they decide to kidnap two girls and hold them for ransom so they can buy plane tickets back home."

"First class tickets," Mr. Henley said.

Mrs. Henley laughed. "Right. First class. Not coach or business class."

"Then we stumbled across Schloss Mueller and knew it would be the perfect place for something in the movie. It's a gorgeous old castle."

"We did some asking around in the village and they told us a bit about the place. That's why we're here now."

"And the *Christkindlmarkt* part?" Mrs. Mason asked.

"The girls already know about this part. We

came up with this in the gondola."

"You're going to use a *Krampus* to snatch the girls," Eva said.

Mrs. Henley nodded and smiled.

"Because it's easy to peel off the mask, throw a coat over the costume, and toss the broom," Brooke added and smiled.

Mr. Henley gave her a funny look. "Did we come up with that idea in the gondola?"

Eva giggled. "And then you're going to hide the girls in the cemetery."

"But the girls hide from you, instead. And when one of them sneezes, you think it's a cat sneezing," Brooke added.

"What?" Mrs. Henley burst out laughing. "So you girls were in the cemetery, too?" She looked at her husband. "I think we're going to have to hire these girls to give us ideas for the plot. They're two steps ahead of us."

Eva and Brooke laughed too. Finally, they felt safe.

"This is turning out to be a perfect day," Brooke said.

"No," Eva said. "It won't be perfect until tomorrow—"

"When your mom and dad get here," Brooke finished her friend's sentence. "You're right. Today is only mostly perfect."

Car tires crunched in the snow outside.

Drew cleared his throat. "Yes, it'll be perfect when all of our family is together," he said. He opened the massive front door and disappeared outside.

"Were you expecting more company, Herr Mueller?" Mrs. Mason asked.

He shook his head and looked confused.

Car doors slammed. A car trunk opened and shut. They could hear voices.

Eva perked up. "*Mutter? Vater?* They're here already!" She dashed outside. Brooke heard her squeal and then shout, *"Sie sind zu hause!"* You're home.

Eva pulled her mom and dad through the door. "They're here! They're really here." The room became a flurry of hugs and kisses and handshakes.

Drew stepped in the door carrying some suitcases. An older woman came in behind him. No one noticed her for a few moments with all the excitement of finally meeting Eva's mom and dad.

She stayed quiet through all of it. And then Herr Mueller noticed her. *"Guten Abend.* I don't believe we've had the pleasure of meeting."

The woman looked vaguely familiar to Brooke. She stood almost as tall as Herr Mueller and had his same lean body. Her gray hair curled softly around her face, and she had the same sky-blue eyes as Eva. She smiled. In that moment, Brooke knew exactly who this stranger was.

The whole room seemed to know at once.

*"Vater,* we brought a special guest with us,"

Eva's dad said. "When we heard your story last summer about the secret room, we knew we had to make this happen."

"Eva?" Herr Mueller whispered. "Eva Mueller?"

The woman smiled again and nodded. "I'm Eva Mueller Bender, your long lost cousin and Drew's grandmother." She held out her hands to Herr Mueller. "And you must be Rudolf. Finally, we meet."

Herr Mueller squeezed her hands and kissed her cheek. "Welcome home, Eva. Welcome home."

From then on, it was crazy awesome. Everyone hugged and kissed and shook hands some more. They talked and laughed and even cried, but the tears were happy ones.

"I can't believe I'm finally back in Schloss Mueller," Mrs. Bender said. "I've dreamed so many times of this place." She looked up at the vast space above her and down at the ballerina in the floor. "I missed Austria. I never thought I'd see this again. And

I never thought I'd meet you, Rudolf. Or you, Eva. I can't believe I have a great niece named after me."

The young Eva gave the old Eva a big hug. "And I can't believe I've finally met you. I'm glad you finally came back to Schloss Mueller," she said to the woman. "I have something for you." She slipped the chain and the heart-shaped silver locket off her neck. It was the one the girls had found in the secret room the first time they played there.

"Here." Eva held it out to her great aunt. "You left this in the secret playroom when your dad took you away from Schloss Mueller."

Mrs. Bender took the locket. She carefully opened the latch and stared at the pictures. Now the tears really came. She kissed Eva on the cheek. "I really am home now."

Brooke and Eva looked at each other.

"And now finally, everything really is perfect," Eva said.

# Mystery of the Thief in the Night

## Chapter One

Ka-BOOM!!

Izzy Bennett jumped a mile high.

Well, she didn't actually jump—and she certainly didn't jump a mile high—since she was sound asleep when the racket woke her. But her eyes flew wide open.

Katie Kitty, Izzy's cat, was the one who jumped a mile high. "Meowwwwww!" she screeched. She tumbled off the bed and leapt into the cubby below Izzy's berth.

"Scaredy-cat," Izzy muttered. "We're just tacking." Her own heart pounded too, though. She turned over and reached down into the cubby to scratch behind Katie's ears. It calmed both of them a bit. In a minute, Katie started purring softly.

The water whooshed against the side of the sailboat. Izzy closed her eyes and tried to go back to sleep, but it wasn't going to happen. They were on a tack that made the boat tilt at an angle. Izzy felt like she was going to roll off her bed.

Back home in Seattle, she never had to worry about falling out of bed because the house leaned over.

There was nothing normal about life on a boat.

Izzy sighed and climbed out of her berth. She pulled on a sweatshirt and sweatpants and carefully made her way to the steps up to the cockpit. When they were at sea, it felt like they lived in one of those crazy circus funhouses. Nothing was flat. Everything was at an angle.

Her dad was in the cockpit reading. She crawled up on the seat with him and snuggled close. He put his arm around her. "Izzy Lizzie. What are you doing up at two o'clock in the morning?"

"Katie Kitty woke me. She didn't like the noise

from the tack." She didn't mention she didn't like the noise either. Izzy was always a little nervous at sea. Well, more than a little. But there wasn't any way to get their boat from one place to the next without going to sea. She tried not to think about all the scary things that could happen. Like hitting another boat or even a whale. Or being knocked over by a humongous wave and then sinking fast. Or getting lost. She had a lonnnggggg list that got longer on every trip.

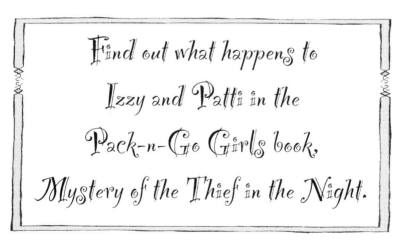

Find out what happens to Izzy and Patti in the Pack-n-Go Girls book, Mystery of the Thief in the Night.

# Meet More Pack-n-Go Girls!

*Discover Australia with Wendy and Chloe!*

**Mystery of the Min Min Lights**

It's hot. It's windy. It's dusty. It's the Australian outback. Wendy Lee arrives from California. She's lucky to meet Chloe Taylor, who invites Wendy to their sheep station. It sounds like fun except that someone is stealing the sheep. And the thief just might be something as crazy as a UFO.

*Discover Brazil with Sofia and Júlia!*

**Mystery of the Troubled Toucan**

Nine-year-old Sofia Diaz's world is coming apart. So is the rickety old boat that carries her far up the Rio Negro river in Brazil. Crocodiles swim in the dark waters. Spiders scurry up the twisted tree trunks. And a crazy toucan screeches a warning. It chases Sofia and Júlia, her new friend, deep into the steamy rainforest. There they stumble upon a shocking discovery. Don't miss the second Brazil book, *Mystery of the Lazy Loggerhead*.

# Meet More Pack-n-Go Girls!

## *Discover Thailand with Jess and Nong May!*

**Mystery of the Golden Temple**

Nong May and her family have had a lot of bad luck lately. When nine-year-old Jess arrives in Thailand and accidentally breaks a special family treasure, it seems to only get worse. It turns out the treasure holds a secret that could change things forever!

## *Discover Mexico with Izzy and Patti!*

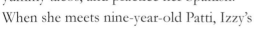

**Mystery of the Thief in the Night**

Izzy's family sails into a quiet lagoon in Mexico and drops their anchor. Izzy can't wait to explore the pretty little village, eat yummy tacos, and practice her Spanish. When she meets nine-year-old Patti, Izzy's thrilled. Now she can do all that and have a new friend to play with too. Life is perfect. At least it's perfect until they realize there's a midnight thief on the loose! Don't miss the second Mexico book, *Mystery of the Disappearing Dolphin.*

# What to Know Before You Go!

## Christmas Traditions in Austria

Every country has special traditions and foods with important holidays. Christmas in Austria is a favorite time of the year, both for Austrians and visitors. When you go to Austria at Christmastime, look for these traditions.

## Christkindlmarkt

Austria is full of Christmas markets, or *Christkindlmärkte*. It's such a favorite tradition that many US cities also have them. An Austrian *Christkindlmarkt* begins the first week of Advent, or four weeks before Christmas. The market will have lots of little booths that sell homemade jam and honey, tea, baked treats like pretzels or cookies, grilled bratwursts, and *Gluhwein*. You'll also find Christmas decorations, handcrafted wooden dishes, candleholders, needlework, and Advent calendars. You'll often hear groups singing or musical groups playing. The best *Christkindlmärkte* touch all the senses: sight, sound, taste, touch, and smell.

## Krampus

In the US, we have the tradition of Santa Claus, who gives presents based on whether children are good or bad. Austrians have the *Krampus*, who is a very scary beast-like creature. The tradition is that the *Krampus* punishes naughty children and will even capture them and take them away. You'll also see people dressed in *Krampus* costumes at Christmas markets, or *Christkindlmärkte*, especially on the evening of December 5, which is the eve of Saint Nicholas Day. They wear scary masks, carry chains and bells or brooms and stroll through the streets to beat the naughtiness out of children. These days, many groups dressed in *Krampus* costumes go through different villages at the same time. So you might see as many as a hundred of these devils. They playfully scare adults and children alike.

# Saint Nicholas Eve, December 5

On the evening of December 5, Saint Nicholas visits children's homes. He may bring a *Krampus* with him. Saint Nicholas reads from his very large book, which lists the ways the children have misbehaved. He also reads some nice things he heard about the children over the last year. Children say a prayer or a poem and are rewarded with treats such as oranges, chocolates, and peanuts. Of course, the *Krampus* will shake his chain when listening to misbehavior. As you can imagine, some children are afraid of the *Krampus* and dread his visit.

## Christmas Trees and Gift Exchanges

Austrians also have a tradition of Christmas trees. The door to the room is closed all day on Christmas Eve to allow the *Christkind* to decorate in secret. In the evening after dinner, a tinkling bell is heard. Everyone comes into the room to see the beautiful tree. It may be decorated with cookies that are wrapped in paper, chocolate ornaments, and lit candles. This is also the time Austrians exchange Christmas gifts, which are nicely spread out under the tree.

# Vanillekipferl

*Vanillekipferl* is a favorite Austrian Christmas cookie. They're shaped into little quarter moons, or crescents, and then baked. It takes a few days for them to get crumbly, which is how Austrians like to eat them!

## Recipe for Vanillekipferl

**Ingredients** *(If you make this recipe, be sure to get an adult to help you.)*:

1. Using a mixer, combine together:
   - 1 cup butter, softened   • 2 tablespoons sugar   • ⅛ teaspoon salt

2. Add and knead into a soft dough:
   - 2½ cups flour   • ½ cup ground almonds

3. Cover the dough and put it into the refrigerator for about an hour.

4. Divide the dough into four parts. Roll each part into a long rope about ½" thick. Cut the ropes into pieces that are 2-3" long. Curve each piece into a quarter moon shape. Place the cookies on an ungreased cookie sheet.

5. Preheat the oven to 325 degrees. Bake the cookies for 12-15 minutes, or until they are a light brown.

6. While the cookies are still hot, toss them in a small bowl of powdered sugar. Let the cookies cool completely on a rack.

Put them in a sealed container and hide them for a couple of days so they don't all get eaten before they get crumbly! The recipe makes about 2½ dozen cookies.

# Say It in German!

Grüß Gott!

| English | German | German Pronunciation |
|---------|--------|---------------------|
| Hello | Hallo | Hahl-lō |
| Hello (Good day) | Grüß Gott | Grōss gŏt |
| Good day | Guten Tag | Gū-těn tahg |
| Good morning | Guten Morgen | Gū-těn morgen |
| Good night | Guten Abend | Gū-těn ah-bend |
| Hi | Hi/Tag | Tahg |
| Goodbye | Auf Wiedersehen | Auf vē-der-zāhn |
| Bye | Tschuess | Tchoos |
| Please | Bitte | Bĭ-tah |
| Thank you (very much) | Danke (schön)/ (Vielen Dank) | Dahn-kah (feel-en dahnk) |
| Excuse me | Entschuldigen Sie mich | Ěnt-shū-lĭ-gěn zee mĭck |
| Yes/No | Ja/Nein | Yah/Nine |
| Enjoy the meal | Guten Appetit | Gū-těn a-pě-teet |
| Grandfather | Grossvater | Grōss-vahter |
| Mrs./Miss | Frau/Fräulein | Frow/Frow-line |
| Mr. | Herr | Hair |
| Castle | Schloss | Shlōss |
| Sweetheart | Liebling | Leeb-lĭng |

| English | German | German Pronunciation |
|---|---|---|
| Run | Lauf | Lauf |
| Hurry | Schnell | Schnell |
| Mother | Mutter | Mūt-ah |
| Father | Vater | Faht-ah |
| Christmas Market | Christkindlmarkt | Krĭs-kĭnt-markt |
| Almond | Mandeln | Mĕn-delln |
| Silent Night | Stille Nacht | Vee-fel/vee-fēlah |
| Cemetery | Friedhof | Freed-hof |
| Come | Komm | Kom |
| 0 | Null | Null |
| 1 | Eins | Īnz |
| 2 | Zwei | Zvī |
| 3 | Drei | Drī |
| 4 | Vier | Fear |
| 5 | Fünf | Funf |
| 6 | Sechs | Zĕchs |
| 7 | Sieben | Zēbĕn |
| 8 | Acht | Ahcht |
| 9 | Neun | Noin |
| 10 | Zehn | Zāne |

Do you speak German? If so, you might notice *Herr* Mueller is used in some places where the correct German form is *Herrn* Mueller. So English readers aren't confused, Herr Mueller is used throughout as the character's name.

**My Austrian Trip Planner**

**Where to go:** _____

_____

_____

_____

_____

_____

_____

_____

_____

_____

_____

_____

_____

_____

_____

_____

_____

**What to do:** _____

_____

_____

_____

_____

_____

_____

_____

_____

_____

_____

_____

_____

_____

_____

_____

_____

My Austrian Trip Planner

**Things I want to pack:**

_____

_____

_____

_____

_____

_____

_____

_____

_____

_____

_____

_____

_____

_____

_____

_____

# Friends to send postcards to:

My Austrian Trip Planner

_____

_____

_____

_____

_____

_____

_____

_____

_____

_____

_____

_____

_____

_____

# Thank you to the following Pack-n-Go Girls:

Maia Caprice
Lisa Muehlfellner
Abby Rice
Sarah Travis
Caroline Yoder

Thank you also to Keri Caprice, Patrice Dunbar, Karoline Muehlfellner, Ashley Rice, Andrea Rieger, and Jeannie Sheeks.

*And a special thanks to my Pack-n-Go Girls co-founder,*
*Lisa Travis, and our husbands, Steve Diller and Rich Travis,*
*who have been along with us on this adventure.*

**Janelle Diller** has always had a passion for writing. As a young child, she wouldn't leave home without a pad and pencil just in case her novel hit her and she had to scribble it down quickly. She eventually learned good writing takes a lot more time and effort than this. Fortunately, she still loves to write. She's especially lucky because she also loves to travel. She's explored over 45 countries for work and play and can't wait to land in the next new country. It doesn't get any better than writing stories about traveling. Janelle and her husband split their time between a sailboat in Mexico and a house in Colorado.

**Adam Turner** has been working as a freelance illustrator since 1987. He has illustrated coloring books, puzzle books, magazine articles, game packaging, and children's books. He's loved to draw ever since he picked up his first pencil as a toddler. Instead of doing the usual two-year-old thing of chewing on it or poking his eye out  with it, he actually put it on paper and thus began the journey. Adam also loves to travel and has had some crazy adventures. He's swum with crocodiles in the Zambezi, jumped out of a perfectly good airplane, and even fished for piranha in the Amazon. It's a good thing drawing relaxes his nerves! Adam lives in Arizona with his wife and their daughter.

# Pack-n-Go Girls Online

Dying to know when the next Pack-n-Go Girls book will be out? Want to learn more German or how to yodel? Trying to figure out what to pack for your next trip? Looking for cool family travel tips? Interested in some fun learning activities about Austria to use at home or at school while you are reading *Mystery at the Christmas Market*?

- Check out our website:
  **www.packngogirls.com**

- Follow us on Twitter:
  **@packngogirls**

- Like us on Facebook:
  **facebook.com/packngogirls**

- Follow us on Instagram:
  **packngogirlsadventures**

- Discover great ideas on Pinterest:
  **Pack-n-Go Girls**

Made in the USA
Middletown, DE
30 September 2017